WEDDINGS UNDER ·A· WESTERN SKY

LISA PLUMLEY

ELIZABETH LANE

KATE WELSH

TORONTO NEW YORK LONDON
AMSTERDAM PARIS SYDNEY HAMBURG
STOCKHOLM ATHENS TOKYO MILAN MADRID
PRAGUE WARSAW BUDAPEST AUCKLAND

ISBN-13: 978-0-373-29691-0

WEDDINGS UNDER A WESTERN SKY
Copyright © 2012 by Harlequin Books S.A.

The publisher acknowledges the copyright holders
of the individual works as follows:

Recycling programs
for this product may
not exist in your area.

THE HAND-ME-DOWN BRIDE
Copyright © 2012 by Elizabeth Lane

THE BRIDE WORE BRITCHES
Copyright © 2012 by Kate Welsh

SOMETHING BORROWED, SOMETHING TRUE
Copyright © 2012 by Lisa Plumley

This edition published by arrangement with Harlequin Books S.A.

For questions and comments about the quality of this book
please contact us at Customer_eCare@Harlequin.ca.

® and TM are trademarks of the publisher. Trademarks indicated with
® are registered in the United States Patent and Trademark Office, the
Canadian Trade Marks Office and in other countries.

www.Harlequin.com

Printed in U.S.A.

CONTENTS

THE HAND-ME-DOWN BRIDE

Elizabeth Lane

To the Fillies

Chapter One

❧❧❧

Buffalo Bend, Montana
April 29, 1876

Arabella Spencer huddled under the dripping eave of Brophy's Feed and Mercantile where the stage had let her off with her trunk. Rain had churned the deserted street into a quagmire of mud and manure. The muck had ruined her new kidskin shoes and wasn't doing much for her disposition. After more than twenty minutes of waiting, she was wet, worried and getting madder by the second.

Charles, her fiancé, had certainly known she was coming. He'd mailed her the tickets three months ago, with a promise to meet the stage and drive her to his new ranch. Only the thought of their wedding, and the fine home he'd refurbished especially for her, had sustained her on the grueling journey by train and stagecoach, all the way from Boston to Buffalo Bend. Now she was here at last, bruised, chilled and bone-weary, with Grandma Peabody's wedding dress packed into her trunk.

The bride had arrived. So where was her groom?

True, the stage had been delayed two hours by a broken

wheel. But that was no excuse for Charles not to be here—especially given that she had no place to get out of the rain. Brophy's Feed and Mercantile, which appeared to be the only store in this ramshackle excuse for a town, had long since closed for the night. There wasn't a hotel in sight, or even a restaurant; and the church at the street's far end looked as dark as a tomb.

Only the saloon across the street showed any sign of life. Lamplight filtered through gray sheets of rain. Occasional bursts of laughter and the wheeze of a concertina drifted over the drone of the storm.

Arabella shivered beneath her damp woolen traveling cloak. The thought of shelter was tempting. But she'd have to leave her precious trunk behind and wade through ankle-deep mud to cross the street. In any case, well-bred young ladies simply did not venture into saloons—not even in a deluge fit to float Noah's ark.

A flicker of movement across the street caught her eye. Someone had just come out of the saloon. Was it Charles? Had he been waiting for her in that disreputable place?

But the man who stepped into the street was too tall and too broad-shouldered to be her fiancé. Charles was of average stature. The figure striding toward her, wearing a bulky sheepskin coat, loomed like a giant against the roiling sky.

Arabella shrank into the doorway. If the man meant her harm, she'd have no place to run. But she could kick and bite and scream for all she was worth. If it came to that, she vowed, she wouldn't go down without a fight.

He stopped a pace away from her. Close up, he wasn't as huge as she'd first thought. But he was big enough—six foot four, by her reckoning. His face was obscured by rain streaming off the broad brim of his hat.

"Miss Arabella Spencer?" His voice was like the rumble

of an iron wheel over a graveled road. "I was told to look for a redhead, so I'm guessing you're the one."

Staring up at him, she nodded.

"McIntyre's the name. I've come to fetch you to the ranch. Wait here, and I'll bring the buckboard around."

He thrust something toward her. Realizing it was an oilskin, Arabella seized it eagerly and wrapped it over her damp cloak. Before she could utter a proper thank-you, the man had melted into the rain.

Moments later he reappeared from behind the store, driving an open rig behind a team of sturdy bays. The back was filled with some kind of bulky cargo covered by a canvas tarpaulin. There was one bench seat in front, with nothing to shelter its occupants from the rain.

For heaven's sake, if Charles couldn't come himself, why couldn't he at least have sent a covered buggy?

McIntyre halted the horses, climbed to the ground and came around the rig—a buckboard, he'd called it, though it was more like a wagon, drawn by two horses instead of one. Hefting Arabella's trunk as if it weighed nothing, he slid it under the canvas in back.

"Where's my fiancé, Charles Middleton?" Arabella demanded. "Is he all right?"

"Far as I know, he's fine." McIntyre's big hands caught her waist and boosted her onto the bench as if she were no bigger than a child.

"Then why didn't he come to meet me?"

"Spring's a busy time for ranchers. I had to drive to town for feed and salt, so he asked me to pick you up." He climbed onto the bench beside her. "It's a long ride. Too bad I hadn't counted on the rain, or on the stage being late."

As if that had been *her* fault! "Well, at least you got to spend a couple of hours in the saloon," she sniffed.

"Uh-huh. Had a drink and won fifty dollars in a game

of five-card stud." His hands flicked the reins. The wagon plowed forward through the sticky mud.

Struck by a sudden realization, she stared at him. "Wait— you were in the saloon when the stage arrived. You must've heard it stop, and you knew I'd be getting off. Why on earth did you leave me standing outside in the rain?"

He shrugged. "I was holding a royal flush."

"Of all the oafish, inconsiderate—" Arabella squelched the rest of her tirade. McIntyre didn't strike her as any kind of gentleman. If a woman got on his nerves, there was no telling what he might do. She could find herself standing alone in the mud.

She resolved to hold her tongue for now. But she planned to have a word with Charles about McIntyre's behavior. Such insolence! The man should be dismissed from service at once.

They left the town behind. There appeared to be a road of sorts, but it was even rougher than the stage route from Laramie which, after five days of constant jouncing, had left her black-and-blue. The wagon swayed and groaned, its wheels lurching over rocks and sagging through puddles of mud. Rain poured down in a steady deluge. Peering out from under the oilskin, Arabella could see clumps of sagebrush on either side, but whatever lay beyond that was obscured by darkness.

At least the horses seemed to know where they were going. They plodded along at a calm pace, ignoring the rain that sheeted down their sides. McIntyre sat hunched over the reins, water drizzling off his hat and streaming down his sheepskin coat. His very silence was an affront, as if he didn't consider her worth the bother of polite conversation. Clearly, for whatever reason, the man didn't like her.

At least she could try to discover why.

"How long have you been working for Charles?" she asked.

"I don't." He didn't bother to look at her.

"You don't work for him?"

"No."

So much for asking Charles to fire the man. "You're a friend of his, then?"

McIntyre didn't reply.

"A neighbor?"

"You could say that."

"Then you'll be my neighbor, too! I suppose Charles told you we were going to be married."

Did McIntyre flinch beneath his coat? Maybe she'd just imagined it, Arabella thought as she waited for the response that never came. Where were his manners?

"Did you hear me?" she demanded. "I said Charles and I were going to be—"

"I heard you." His voice was a growl. What was eating at the man? Arabella was tempted to give him a lecture in courtesy. But that, she sensed, would be a waste of breath.

She'd done her best to make pleasant conversation. But if her driver wanted to be rude, she wouldn't trouble him further. Instead she would pass the time as she had on the train and inside the dusty, rattling stagecoach—thinking about Charles, their wedding and their future.

She had known Charles Middleton all her life. They'd grown up next door to each other in Boston. Everyone who knew them had assumed they'd marry one day. When Charles's aging father had died last year, his older brother, Frank, had inherited the family estate and ship-building business. Charles had used his own generous inheritance to buy a Montana cattle ranch complete with a two-story house, corrals and outbuildings, and a herd of five thousand cattle.

"I'll send for you next spring, dearest," he'd promised her at the railway station. "While we're apart I'll have a crew remodeling the house into a home to make you proud—a home where we can raise our children and live happily for the rest of our days."

Charles wasn't the most reliable of men—his enthusiasm often overran his better instincts. But in this case, he had kept his word. After the tickets arrived, Arabella had passed the long winter days sewing her trousseau and planning her wedding. She wasn't sure what life would be like on a Montana ranch. But as long as Charles was there, she knew she'd be happy.

She imagined standing before the preacher, wearing Grandma Peabody's wedding dress and gazing up into Charles's tender blue eyes as she spoke her vows. *I, Arabella, take thee, Charles—*

"Damnation!" McIntyre's curse shattered her reverie. The wagon had halted, the way broken by a four-foot drop-off above a flowing torrent of muddy water.

McIntyre purpled the air with half-mouthed curses. "Damn, blasted bridge is washed out. If we can't ford the creek we'll be stuck here waiting." Turning, he thrust the reins into Arabella's hands. "Can you handle a team?"

"I've driven a chaise."

"That'll have to do. Hold the horses steady till I get back." He vaulted to the ground and strode off into the storm.

Arabella peered through the murk. Fear uncoiled in her stomach and crawled up into her throat. McIntyre was probably looking for a shallow place to cross. But the water looked fast and deep, and so wide she couldn't see the far side of it. What if he lost his footing and was swept away? What would she do out here alone if he didn't come back?

Minutes crawled past. The horses danced and snorted. She gripped the reins hard, praying the skittish beasts wouldn't bolt. She didn't want to die out here in the cold, dark rain. She wanted to make it to the ranch, marry Charles and spend happy years raising his children.

The sound of the water was a dull roar. Was it deep enough to

drown a man? Panic ran an icy finger up her spine. "McIntyre!" Her shout was lost in the storm. "Where are you?"

"Right here." He appeared on the far side of the wagon, tossed the branch he was holding into the back and climbed onto the seat. His trousers and boots were coated with mud.

"Did you find a way across?" she asked.

"Nothing sure. The smart thing would be to wait here till morning. We'll have daylight then, and the water should be down."

"Oh, no!" Arabella responded with a horrified gasp. "We can't possibly do that! Think of my reputation! Think how Charles will worry! We simply must go on!"

McIntyre exhaled raggedly, shaking his head. "I had a feeling you'd say that. There's a place upstream that might do for a ford. But if you get a soaking, don't say I didn't warn you."

"I'm soaked now!" she huffed.

Without another word he took the reins, backed up and swung the team to the left. The wagon lurched over rocks and crashed through clumps of sagebrush, stopping fifty yards upstream at the crest of a sandy incline that sloped down to the swollen creek.

McIntyre studied the roiling current. "We'd still be better off waiting for daylight. I know what you're thinking, but this is Montana, not Boston. Nobody here's going to give a damn about your precious reputation. As for your virtue…" His eyes flickered toward her, and when he spoke again his voice was dry and cold. "Lady, you've got nothing to worry about there."

Arabella's chin went up. "Believe me, if you did give me any cause for concern, my fiancé would have you shot."

Something between a snarl and a curse rumbled in his throat. "What the hell," he snapped, "let's go."

His big hands urged the horses down the bank. Stopping them at the water's edge, he handed her the reins. "I'll be

going ahead to test the bottom and lead the team," he said. "All you'll need to do is hold on and keep them from moving too fast. All right?"

Arabella nodded, feeling a vague chill of fear. The water looked swift and deep. Maybe she should tell McIntyre she'd changed her mind. But the idea of admitting he was right stuck in her craw. And the thought of Charles, waiting with open arms, sealed her resolve. She held her tongue as he stripped off his coat, lifted the branch from the bed of the wagon and swung to the ground.

Without a backward glance, he walked to the head of the team and placed himself between the two husky bays. Even next to his horses, McIntyre looked powerful. He glanced from one animal to the other, as if reassuring them. Then with a voiced command Arabella could barely hear, he urged them into the flooded creek.

Knee-deep, then hip-deep, he eased forward. One hand held the branch, which he used to probe the depth of the creek bed in front of him. The other hand controlled the horses, moving from one to the other. Arabella gripped the reins as the wagon swayed into the current. McIntyre was trusting her with his life, she realized. If she let the horses bolt they could drag him under and trample or drown him.

The water was over the wheel hubs, but the spring-mounted bed of the buckboard wagon remained dry. Arabella thought of Grandma Peabody's silk wedding dress. She had wrapped the precious garment in oilcloth, but little good that would do if the trunk slipped into the creek and washed away. She willed herself to focus on holding the horses. They were making slow but steady progress. Now, through the rainy darkness, she could make out a stand of willows on the far side. They were almost there.

"Whoa!" McIntyre's shout rang out above the rush of the current. Arabella jerked back on the reins, but not fast enough.

As the wheels rolled forward, the rig sagged toward the right front corner and groaned to a halt.

McIntyre was cursing. "Damned hole. We're stuck."

"Can we get loose?"

"Not likely. All we can do is try. Hold the horses steady." He left his place at the head of the team and made his way around to the sagging side of the wagon. Taking the branch he'd used to test the creek bottom, he wedged it behind the stuck wheel. Keeping the reins taut, Arabella watched him.

"As long as you're using a lever, it would help to have a fulcrum," she said.

He glared up at her with murder in his eyes. "It would help to have a lot of things. But right now I'm up to my ass in muddy water and it's all I can do to push on this damned wheel. So I'll thank you to just keep your pretty mouth shut and do what I tell you. All right?"

"All right," Arabella snapped. She'd only meant to help. But clearly McIntyre wasn't the sort to take advice from a mere woman.

"When I push, you ease the team forward. But not too hard, mind you, or the wheel will break and spill everything overboard, including you. Understand?"

"Go ahead. I'm ready." She gripped the reins, pretending they were wrapped around his neck.

He braced against the limb, water rippling around his lean hips. "Now!" he grunted, pushing with his full weight.

Arabella flicked the reins, keeping them tight. The horses leaned forward in their traces, their massive shoulders bulging. The wagon creaked fearfully with the strain but the wheels didn't move.

"Whoa!" McIntyre straightened, breathing hard. "Give me a minute, and we'll try it again."

Arabella risked a furtive look past her shoulder. He was soaked with muddy water, his denim work shirt clinging to

his muscular frame. His hat was gone, his hair wet and flat against his head. His craggy features looked as if they'd been chiseled from living rock.

McIntyre could never be called handsome. The raw, masculine aura that hung about him was more frightening than appealing. He was like an untamed beast. Yes, that was the word for him. Untamed.

He took a deep breath. "Ready?"

"Ready." As he shoved his weight against the branch, she coaxed the team forward. The wagon strained and quivered like a living thing. Just when she thought it might shift free, Arabella heard a snap and a curse. She stopped the horses. McIntyre was standing next to the mired wheel, the broken branch in his hand.

"That's it," he growled. "This damned rig's not going anywhere till morning."

Her heart sank. "You mean we're just going to sit here all night in the middle of the creek?"

He tossed the broken branch into the flood. "Horses can't stand in the water that long. I'll have to unhitch them and lead them to the bank. We can ride the team the rest of the way home. At first light I'll come back with some men and haul the rig out."

"Fine. But I can't leave my trunk."

"Your blasted trunk weighs sixty pounds. I'll get it tomorrow and drop it off for you."

"My grandmother's wedding dress is in that trunk. I'm not leaving without it."

His eyes narrowed to wolfish slits. "Fine, woman. I'll take the horses home and you can sit here all night with your trunk. If any Blackfeet come by you can pour them a cup of tea!"

"Blackfeet?" Arabella's heart lurched into her throat. "You mean *Indians*?"

"They've been known to wander this way. Most likely

they'd have enough sense to stay home on a night like this, but you never know..." Letting the words hang, he sloshed forward through the water and began unbuckling the first horse from the traces.

Without a second glance at Arabella, he led the horse to the far bank, tied it in the willows and started back. The current was strong enough to carry a man away. Without support, it was all McIntyre could do to keep his footing. Watching him struggle, Arabella knew she'd never make it to shore without his help.

Would he really leave her? She wouldn't put it past him. McIntyre was, without doubt, the most exasperating man she'd ever met. But he was right about one thing—there was no way to get her heavy trunk ashore or carry it on a horse. For now, it would have to stay on the wagon. The only question was whether or not she would stay with it.

What if the flood rose and swept the trunk into the water; or what if someone came by and took it? She couldn't imagine what an Indian would do with Grandma Peabody's wedding gown, but the thought did give her a sudden idea.

Looping the reins over the seat, she scrambled into the back of the wagon, found the trunk under the canvas and opened it with the key she wore on a ribbon around her neck. Rummaging through the tightly packed layers of clothing, she lifted out the precious bundle—the one thing in the trunk that couldn't be replaced.

"Change your mind?" McIntyre had made it back to the wagon and had started unbuckling the second horse.

"You knew I would! Indians, indeed! Why not man-eating tigers?" Arabella locked the trunk and shoved it back under the sheltering canvas. "My grandmother's wedding dress is coming with me. Rain or shine, I mean to be married in it!"

She'd expected a sharp retort, but McIntyre had turned away. He didn't look up until she'd returned to the front of

the wagon. "I'll have to carry you to the horse." He moved to stand below her. "Let's go."

Arabella stood on the edge of the wagon, clutching her precious bundle. Seized by hesitation, she stared down at the rushing water.

"Stop wasting time. I'll catch you. Trust me."

Trust was the last thing Arabella felt. Few things, she suspected, would give the man more pleasure than dropping her in the creek. But she had little choice. Gulping back her fear, she leaned over the water and willed herself to let go.

He caught her handily, one arm supporting her back, the other cradling her legs. Through his wet clothes, his chest was as solid as a granite wall. She could feel the strong, steady pulsing of his heart.

Gazing up at his face she noticed, for the first time, a slashing white scar running from his cheekbone to the corner of his mouth. Had he been in the war—or maybe fought Indians? He was an intriguing man, and she couldn't deny the curiosity she felt. But something told her he wouldn't welcome personal questions.

McIntyre held her as if she were covered in poison ivy. Arabella could sense the resistance in him. He strode toward the horse, pushing through the current as if he couldn't wait to get rid of her. Clearly she made him uncomfortable. But why? What had she ever done to him? Maybe he had something against women—or against redheads.

The second horse was still harnessed to the wagon. Clutching the bundled wedding dress, Arabella clambered from McIntyre's arms onto its back. She'd never ridden astride, but this was no time to be fussy. Rucking her skirts above her knees, she straddled the slippery barrel of its body. Her free hand kept a death grip on the harness. All she wanted was to be on solid ground again.

"Hang on." McIntyre climbed back into the wagon. He

found his sheepskin coat, rolled it tightly and slung it over his shoulder. Then he reached under the bench and lifted a rifle from its hiding place. Maybe he hadn't been fooling about Indians after all.

He was still in the wagon when it happened. A twisted piece of broken limb came washing down the flooded creek. The limb wasn't large enough to do much damage, but it was headed straight toward the horse.

The nervous animal screamed and bucked. Grabbing the harness with both hands, Arabella managed to stay mounted, but her precious bundle flew out of her grasp and into the fast-flowing water.

"No!" Ignoring safety and common sense, she flung herself off the horse and into the flood after it. Here at the ford, the water wasn't much higher than her waist, but the current was rough and shockingly cold. A dozen yards ahead she could see the yellow oilcloth bundle, bobbing along the stream.

McIntyre was shouting at her, probably swearing a blue streak. Ignoring him, she plunged after her treasure. Not far ahead, a dead alder had washed free of the bank and fallen across the stream. The current had formed an eddy there. She caught glimpses of the bundle as it swirled round and round. Could she reach it before the eddy pulled it under?

She pushed ahead. The water was deeper here, almost up to her armpits. Arabella was no swimmer, but as long as her feet could touch bottom she felt safe enough; and she had almost reached the eddy. The bundle was circling toward her now. She lunged for it. Her fingers touched the slippery oilcloth. Another lunge and she had it. She clasped it close to her chest.

Only then did she realize her feet could no longer feel bottom. She'd been swept into the eddy's powerful current. It was pulling her down. She groped for the fallen tree with

her free hand. The twig she managed to catch snapped off in her fingers.

"Help!" she shouted, but her cry was lost in the muddy water that filled her mouth and blinded her eyes. Her feet thrashed helplessly. She was drowning. This was the end.

Strong arms jerked her out of the current. Her head broke water. She gulped life-giving air.

McIntyre's arm was hooked around her waist. He didn't speak, but she could feel the anger in his taut body as he dragged her back upstream, toward the bank. Incredibly her grandmother's wedding dress was still clasped tightly under her arm. She had saved it after all.

He hauled her ashore and dropped her, none too gently, on the wet grass. From under his dark brows, his deep-set eyes blazed lightning fury. "Not a word, woman!" he snapped. "Not till I get you to where you're going!" He swung back toward the creek where the second horse waited, still harnessed to the wagon. At the water's edge he paused and turned. His expression made Arabella shrivel.

"Damn that wedding dress!" he growled. "I should've let you drown for it!"

By the time they were underway again, the rain had let up. Wrapped in her dripping cloak, Arabella clung to the harness in shivering silence. The horse's broad frame stretched her thighs and chafed her legs to the point of misery. She'd be doing well to get out of bed tomorrow.

McIntyre rode beside her. He'd lost his coat in the plunge to rescue her, but he'd saved the rifle. It lay across his knees, ready if needed. For all Arabella knew, he was thinking of shooting her with it.

She couldn't blame the man for being annoyed. If not for her, he could've left town ahead of the storm and crossed the creek before the bridge washed out. If she hadn't insisted on

fording the creek, the wagon wouldn't have become stuck, and she wouldn't have risked drowning to save her grandmother's wedding dress.

Any man short of sainthood would have been angry. But McIntyre's resentment appeared to go deeper. It was almost as if he'd hated her on sight.

Could he have something against Charles? But if that were so, why had he agreed to pick her up in town?

Never mind the questions, Arabella told herself. When she was safe with Charles, the answers would be made clear enough. She could wait that long.

The moon had come out, painting the rain-washed prairie with silver. It was eerily beautiful. But the most beautiful sight of all was the distant barn, surrounded by sheds and corrals and, on a little knoll, a two-level white frame house with a broad porch, commanding a view of the countryside.

Her heart skipped as they rode closer. She clutched the bundled wedding gown against her chest. The place was just as Charles had described it in his letters. At last she was home.

The hour was late, but lamps lit the porch and the curtained front window. McIntyre stopped the horses at the gate, where a walkway led up to the front steps. Dismounting, he came around to help Arabella to the ground. She was so chilled and sore she could barely stand, but he made no move to assist her the rest of the way to the house.

She did owe him, at least, a token of politeness. "You're welcome to come in," she said. "There's bound to be something to eat, and I'm sure Charles will want to thank you for bringing me home."

He stepped back. For a moment his gaze held hers. In his shadowed eyes she glimpsed impatience, frustration and something else—something unreadable. With a shake of his head, he turned back to the horses, mounted and rode off into the night.

"Arabella!" The front door had opened. Charles stood in the rectangle of light that spilled onto the porch. He hurried down the walk. Numb-footed she stumbled toward him and fell into his arms. For a moment he held her close, then shifted her away, so he could look at her.

"My word, Arabella, what happened?" he gasped. "We were worried about you."

"It's a very long story. Get me warm and I'll tell you." She leaned on him going up the walk. It struck her as odd that he hadn't kissed her, but she could hardly blame him. She must look a fright.

Another figure had appeared in the doorway. Half silhouetted by the lamplight was a tall young woman wearing a man's robe over her nightgown. As she stepped out onto the porch, the light revealed a fresh, pretty face and flaxen braids that hung over her ample breasts.

How thoughtful of Charles, Arabella thought, to hire a female near her own age to be her maid and companion. She mustn't forget to thank him.

Charles paused for a moment, nervously licking his lips. "I sent you a letter," he said. "But I couldn't be sure it would arrive in time to keep you in Boston. That's why I asked McIntyre to wait till the stage showed up."

She stared up at him. "A letter? To *keep* me in Boston after you sent me the stage ticket to come here? Why, Charles, what on earth are you talking about?"

The young blonde woman had come down the steps to stand beside him. She smiled timidly. Charles cleared his throat. "Arabella, dearest," he said, "this is Sally—my wife."

Elizabeth Lane has lived and traveled in many parts of the world, including Europe, Latin America and the Far East, but her heart remains in the American West, where she was born and raised. Her idea of heaven is hiking a mountain trail on a clear fall day. She also enjoys music, animals and dancing. You can learn more about Elizabeth by visiting her website at www.elizabethlaneauthor.com.

As a child, **Kate Welsh** often lost herself in creating make-believe worlds and happily-ever-after tales. Many years later she turned back to creating happy endings when her husband challenged her to write down the stories in her head. A lover of all things romantic, Kate has been writing romance for more than twenty years now. Kate loves hearing from readers, who can reach her on the internet at kate_welsh@verizon.net.

When she's not writing, **Lisa Plumley** loves to spend time with her husband and two children, traveling, hiking, watching classic movies, reading and defending her trivia-game championship. She enjoys hearing from readers, and invites you to contact her via email at lisa@lisaplumley.com, or visit her website at www.lisaplumley.com.

Acclaim for the authors of
Weddings Under a Western Sky

"This tender and ⸻⸻⸻ previous
Western, showca⸻⸻⸻ nsional
characters and ⸻⸻⸻ ⸻lace."
—*RT Bo*⸻

"Lane uses he⸻ ⸻⸻ ⸻⸻-century backdrop and her
knowledge of aviation to her advantage in a lively story
featuring strong-willed characters."
—*RT Book Reviews* on *On the Wings of Love*

KATE WELSH

"Welsh writes of a time in history that's rarely featured
in romance novels—the beginnings of unionization in
the coal mines of the United States. The plot is compelling,
with several subplots that add complexity to the story."
—*RT Book Reviews* on *Questions of Honor*

"A mistaken identity and a deathbed promise throw two
strangers into marriage and mayhem. Welsh's latest is a
heartwarming novel about greed, revenge, love and desire."
—*RT Book Reviews* on *His Californian Countess*

LISA PLUMLEY

"There's plenty of gunslinging, bloodshed and lovemaking
going on from start to finish, which will keep readers turning
pages until the very end."
—*RT Book Reviews* on *Mail-Order Groom*

"How does one spell romance? P-L-U-M-L-E-Y.
Readers are in for a treat with her latest tale, a funny,
lively and often outrageous battle of wills that
will keep readers riveted until the last page."
—*RT Book Reviews* on *The Scoundrel*